$ 20.99

4/16

Rainbow Book

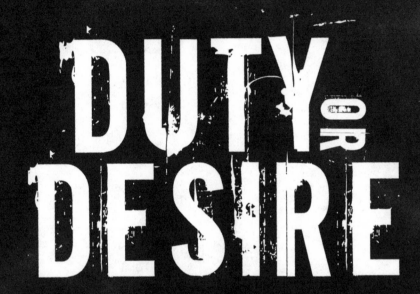

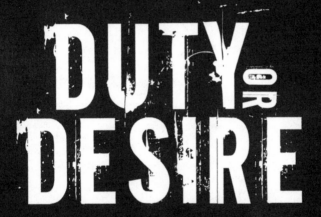

PATRICK JONES & MARSHUNNA CLARK

darbycreek

MINNEAPOLIS

Darby Creek
A division of Lerner Publishing Group, Inc.
241 First Avenue North
Minneapolis, MN 55401 USA

For reading levels and more information, look up this title at
www.lernerbooks.com.

The images in this book are used with the permission of: © Illia Balla/123RF.com (lightning); © iStockphoto.com/yasinguneysu (grass background) © iStockphoto.com/amwu (snake); © iStockphoto.com/Albisoima (blue streaks).

Main body text set in Janson Text LT Std 12/17.5.
Typeface provided by Adobe Systems.

Library of Congress Cataloging-in-Publication Data

The Cataloging-in-Publication Data for *Duty or Desire* is on file at the Library of Congress.
ISBN 978-1-5124-0002-1 (lib. bdg.)
ISBN 978-1-5124-0089-2 (pbk.)
ISBN 978-1-5124-0090-8 (EB pdf)

Manufactured in the United States of America
1 – SB – 12/31/15

Thanks to Billy Shakes for the idea —P.J.

Thank you Yahweh for the gift. A special thanks to my Mom and Dad and Tamiko. —M.L.C.

1

ALEJANDRO

"So Alejandro, how was your vacation up north?" Big Caesar snickers and smirks but there's no smile on my face. I'm flinching like I was getting ready to take a blow to the skull.

"A'right," I mumble, avoiding eye contact. *Don't engage, walk away, follow the plan*, I say to myself, repeating my caseworker's words religiously like I was Mom saying her rosary.

"Rested and ready?" Lorenzo asks.

They stopped me walking to the store. I

could never know when they're around since they do nothing but work a corner and party with thin profits. I'm not surprised I can predict their future, and mine, in that life. Jail. Prison. Coffin. Massive Mom tears. "I gotta go."

Lorenzo grabs my arm, tight, skin on skin.

"We're talking to you." Big Caesar, who of course is a tiny five foot five, stands his twenty-year-old stump of meanness in front of me. "You think you get a pass 'cause you done time?"

"Country club, that's what I heard about Woodland Hills," Lorenzo adds. He wouldn't know the first thing about it, but ain't no sense telling him because they're here to talk, not listen.

Lorenzo squeezes harder. He's got sharp nails. "So, you going back to school or what?" He cares about his distribution, not my graduation.

"I gotta. Condition of my release." *Don't engage, walk away, follow the plan.*

"Whose world you living in, A? Theirs or

ours?" Big Caesar's in my face, as best he can at his height, but acting like he's so much bigger even though he's only three years older. Maybe he thinks that Glock he's got stuck in his waistband makes him some kind of giant.

Cars, city buses, and trucks drive by, creating a city soundtrack to cover my heart beating so loud that it hurts my ears. I need to find the words of my case worker at Woodland Hills, my probation officer at the Juv Justice Center, but mostly Mom to cut through the clatter. I open my mouth, but even though we role-played yesterday, my last day in custody, no sounds emerge. Lorenzo's in my face, nose to nose, so close I smell everything he ate, drank, and smoked today.

"It's business time. Sun's out. We need you," Big C says.

"You owe us," Lorenzo chimes in. Us means the 26ers, our—I mean their—gang.

"Don't surprise me none that he's got no sense of loyalty," Big C says to Lorenzo, though he's glaring at me. "I mean, look how he ditched my baby sis like she was garbage."

"That's over," I say. I guess it was the stack of unanswered letters that Olishia sent me at Woodland that convinced her we were done. She was like her brother: demanding and controlling.

I pull my arm hard, breaking free of Lorenzo's grip, and red blood trickles on my brown skin. Breaking free of the 26ers will be much harder than this, with even more blood. "I'll talk to you later."

"You'll talk to us now." Big C pushes hard against my chest. I take a step back.

"I got nothing to say." I can't take the steps forward I told Mom and the suits I'd make if I let these guys push me around using duty as a weapon.

"You think you're better than us?" Lorenzo asks. Another push. He wants to shove me back to who I was before Woodland Hills. "You better say something."

I step up. With my right hand, I push back my long black hair from my face. With my left index finger, I point to the scar on my forehead that's never going away. "I said everything

when I got beat by those cops 'cause you ran.
I said everything when I said nothing, I didn't
snitch on you. You stayed on the streets. I did
six months."

They look at each other, then Big C nods at
Lorenzo and they let me walk on, this time. I
know there'll be other times, other 26ers, other
temptations, other obstacles. "Later A-hole,"
Lorenzo says in the icy tone of a promise—or
maybe a threat.

I walk head-down, staring at the gray
sidewalk, thinking about their brown faces,
remembering the feel of a black piece. I recall
something somebody said to me in group up at
Woodland: "Alejandro, you got green disease.
You desire cash. You envy those with money,
and you'll do anything to get it." I stare at the
green ink of the 26ers tattoo on my right arm
sprinkled with blood and say aloud, "Don't
engage, walk away, follow the plan."

CHRISSIE

I'm a step in front of my friends, walking backwards, asking Angela about this fool guy at school. We're telling stories on our way home, living in the moment.

"So I say to him, 'why do you call females so many rude names?'" Angela says with sass in her voice. She's got us—me, Lacy, and Robin—hanging on every word. "And he said, 'I don't know. That's just what they are. Dang, why you ask so many questions?'"

Angela does great impersonations of the fool boys she attracts. With her hands making gestures as a guy would, she slows her speech; her lips twist and out of them comes a low tone similar to the guy she is talking about. I met him once at school, and he's like most boys at Northwest: childish. They're all filled with desire, but lacking any sense of respect.

"And I'm looking at this dude like . . . for real?!" Angela's voice raises an octave. And now we're all laughing too loud, sounding like kids ourselves.

"He sounds so stupid," Robin says and then sighs big. "Ya'll it's such a beautiful day! Wish I had my video camera." It's the first nice day after a long Minnesota winter, so everybody's outside.

"You would film ants on a sidewalk." Angela chirps and laughs. Robin slaps her arm. Angela whines in mock pain. My friends are always fake fighting.

"Least I'm not out here talking about adventures with little boys every second!" Robin says. I want to agree with her, but figure it's best if I just stay out of this mess.

"Robin, you can't even take a joke once in a while. Are all wannabe filmmakers that serious?" Angela asks.

My cousin Lacy jumps in. "Angela, you know how sensitive Robin is. Leave her alone." She turns to Robin. "Why don't you use your cell phone to film something?"

Robin and Angela go back and forth, but I'm focused on a paper I have to write when I get home. The weight of the backpack on my back doesn't even compare to what is on my mind. We are seniors. We are about to graduate. The world is at our disposal. But then seeing Robin just standing there with her head down, well, my thoughts can wait.

"Angela, would you like it if someone to called you a wannabe ratchet girl? Stop putting Robin down, and apologize!" I say. Angela narrows her eyes at me, but I don't care.

They make up, and everything's right with the world or at least our little corner of it.

"Chrissie, can I talk to you for a minute?" Robin asks. She motions for me to follow.

We split from Lacy and Angela and walk

down the street. We don't talk until we cross at the light. Whatever Robin's got to say must be a secret. "Is everything okay, hun?" I ask.

She's looking down again, self-consciously picking fuzz off her form-fitting tank. "I hate it when Angela does that. I told her so the other day," Robin confides.

"Good. I'm proud of you! Just don't focus on what other people think, including your girls. Think for you." I tell her.

Robin gives me a big smile. "Thanks Chrissie. You can put on your mom cap quick."

I give her a hug and we walk back toward Lacy and Angela but stop for the "don't walk" light at the intersection. As we wait, a car full of dudes approaches, going way too fast. One of them yells something rude at me. I just roll my eyes. They drive along, and we cross the street.

We're almost back to our girls, walking slow since Robin's telling me about the movie she wants to make, when I hear a car pull up and stop behind us. Not those dudes again, I hope. I don't have time for this. We turn. Car doors open and then close as two cops approach us.

"Do you know who was in that vehicle?" one policeman asks. He's Asian, maybe Hmong. His partner's an older white guy with a scar and scowl. I can tell right away these guys are bad news. I know there's good cops out there, but seems it's guys like these that are always up in our faces for nothing.

"No." The less I say, the better.

"Are you sure you don't know anything?" The Asian cop walks right up to me, in my personal space.

"I do not know, sir." I say the words slow, trying to stay calm. Angela and Lacy stand on the other curb across from us. Robin stays behind, but she's got her cell phone in hand pointing it at me—filming this, I bet.

"I need to see your license, ma'am," says the Asian guy. How old does he think I am?

I cross my arms across my chest. "No. I didn't do anything."

"When an officer tells you to do something, you do it!" the white cop barks at me.

"Look, I don't want any trouble. Are we done here?" I ask, losing patience.

The white office chimes in, "We ask the questions around here. Not you."

Instead of keeping my arms crossed, when I get upset my hands move fast and furious.

"I don't need to show you my license because I didn't do anything. Am I a suspect for a crime? You have no probable cause." I hope Lacy hears me; she'll be proud.

"Leave her alone!" Angela screams from across the street.

Robin says nothing, but Lacy yells at the cops, "I'm calling the police!"

"We are the police," the white cop says with a half-amused smile that doesn't fit the situation.

"Get their badge numbers! This is harassment!" Lacy says, coming on the scene. She's fearless as she stares down the Hmong cop. "I called the non-crooked police." Lacy grew up in the 'burbs, so she don't know that around here, when you call 911 it's 50-50 if you're gonna get somebody to help you or somebody to hurt you.

"Step away from this. We have the situation under control," white cop goes as he pushes

11

by me and swats at Robin's phone, knocking it to the ground. He kicks it away when Robin reaches for it.

"Just give me your license, and we'll let you go home!" the other cop says to me.

"No. If I can't get your name and badge number, you can't get my license!" I take a step back, something I'm not used to doing.

The Asian officer yanks my arm so hard that air jolts out of my lungs. He starts to cuff my wrists, but I try to pull away. He gets me against the police car. All my friends are yelling, but I can't hear 'em well 'cause the Hmong cop is saying, "You should've just done what we said."

I'm five-five, but with meat on my bones. I'm strong and fearless when I need to be, so I push him off me and get away, until the white cop comes at me with a club that smacks me in the face with the force of thunder. I fall to the concrete on my back. I see the clouds move by before my friends' panicked voices grow silent. My body ceases movement as I feel myself escaping into the black that is my head.

ALEJANDRO

"Alex, time for dinner!" Ricardo taps me
too hard on my left leg. He acts like he's
my stepdad, but he's nothing until he mans
up, does his duty, and puts a ring on Mom's
left finger.

"One second." I'm five kills away
from clearing out an enemy squad in *Call
of Duty: Advanced Warfare*. Playing this
game is all I've done since I got home.
School's tomorrow.

"Now." There's a war raging through the headphones, loud enough to drown the words in my head. *Don't engage, walk away, follow the plan.* They teach you these skills inside to say no to your old life on the outs. Stand up for yourself, except with your case manager, probation officer, and parents, then stand in line, be a loyal solider, do your duty. "Alex, I said now!"

When I don't move fast enough, he unplugs the Xbox. I leap to my feet, and Ricardo takes a step back. He's shaped like a bowling pin and I look like a brown bowling ball. I'm about ready to throw a strike when Mom peeks her head in the door. She doesn't need to say a word—she just breaks out that expression that says, "please, Alejandro, not again": eyes down, thin lips turned south. And that's how it makes me feel: down. I say nothing to Ricardo as I walk by him.

At the table, Mom's got a big salad set out. I fill a bowl and take a deep breath. We talked in the car from Woodland, but this is the first family meal since I got home. Well, family that's left. Maria moved to Chicago; Angel moved to Fresno; Hector moved to Iraq, Afghanistan, and now San Diego. Only Raymond stayed in-state. Oak Park Heights. We could visit if he'd ever get out of solitary. He's got fifteen years left.

"So you'll get enrolled back at school tomorrow," Mom says.

"I guess." I chew fast so I can get back to *Call of Duty*.

"You always did so well in school, it's a shame that—" Mom cuts off. There's no reason to relive it. Other than slinging and banging, I was a good student, when I showed up.

"Things will be different this time." Ricardo announces, like he's a part of my life.

"I wish you'd come to church with us," Mom says. "It would do you so much good."

I don't answer so we don't have this argument again, but she doubles down.

"They said at Woodland Hills that you went to church and spoke to the chaplain when—"

"I did that to get out of my room. Inside, everybody says what people want to hear."

"Alex, we want you to be open to the love of Christ, to find meaning in your life . . . to be a responsible member of the family," Ricardo says, trying to stay on Mom's good side. He is good, not great, but better than the others. Mom's got a magnetic personality—although mostly it attracts men who hurt her. But Ricardo doesn't drink (like Mil) or hit her (like José) or both (like Dad), so there's some good in him. "What your mother—"

"Seems to me all these people proclaiming to love some God just end up killing or getting killed." My words echo out of my now empty bowl. "Just like banging, if you ask me."

And that silences the table for a while. Over the rest of the meal, it's a lot of talk about nothing that matters, even though Ricardo keeps trying to talk Twins baseball, like I care.

I'm just about ready to head back to my room when the house phone rings. Ricardo rises, picks it up.

"Alex, it's for you." Ricardo says. *Stop calling me Alex* I want to say, but I let it go. *Don't engage, walk away, follow the plan.* He hands me the phone. My cell's dead and there's been no talk of replacing it, so the landline is it. I look at the 612 number.

"You living in their world or ours?" Big C asks.

I hang up, but I'm not more than two steps away when it rings again. I recognize the number. Same seven numbers, same seven words when I pick up: "You living in their world or ours?" I answer the question by unplugging the phone from the wall. I want to hurl it across the room.

"What's going on?" Ricardo asks. I direct my answer mostly to Mom. She and Ricardo talk about changing the number. Then Ricardo mentions calling the police, and I shut that down. Even the mention of the word *police* causes my head to throb and reopens the wound.

I head into my room, shut and lock the door. I dig into my closet until I find a beaten-up box labeled "baseball cards." It's like being eight years old and innocent again, looking at the names on the cards, except none of these guys wear Twins uniforms anymore. First chance they got, they left for big money.

I lay the cards on the closet floor. The smiling faces of millionaires with brown bats on their shoulders stare up at me as I hear Big C's question ringing in my ears. *You living in their world or ours?* I pull the sleek black .45 from the box; I know there's only one answer. I've got to protect myself however I can as I walk the hard line toward doing my duty, acting like a good man, resisting the temptation to behave like bad boy. "I'm living in *my* world."

4

CHRISSIE

"Sweet . . ."

My cheeks rise up to my eyes, and I hear a faint voice.

"Sweetheart?" Is that Mom?

A groan escapes from the bottom of my throat, and I become aware of a small searing pain in my head. But it's hard to open my eyes for the moment.

"Don't strain yourself, Chrissie Bear." A low baritone voice—my father—tells me. I hate it when my dad calls me that. But I'm so glad to hear him.

"I can open my eyes." I see hospital sheets covering me and three people supporting me. Mom and Dad sit on small hard chairs pushed tight against the bed. Lacy stands behind them.

"How you feel, sweetheart?" Mom asks.

"My head hurts." I reach toward my head and feel the harsh texture of bandage that is bigger than my hand. The bright lights feel like needles in my eyes, but I open them when I hear Lacy's voice. She gazes down at me with a scrunched up face and tears in her eyes.

"When they did that to you . . . I was so scared and angry." Lacy breaks eye contact and looks down. "And helpless."

"It's okay, Lacy . . ." I start.

"No, it isn't. Lacy told us everything," Mom says. "I'm going up to the police department tomorrow. I am telling them I'm going to sue their sorry selves for messing with my baby."

"Mom, look, d- . . . don't . . . make a big deal out of this," I say, still foggy, and as the memory rushes in, I want to push it out, forever.

"Chrissie, what they did was completely out of line," Mom presses. "Look at you." Her voice cracks.

"But—"

"But nothing," comes an angry voice from the corner. Lex. Lacy's brother.

I feel like I'm going to throw up. "I need the bathroom."

Mom lowers the metal railing on the bed. When it hits the rest of the bed, it clangs. To Mom, Dad and Lacy, it sounds like nothing; to me, it's like a gong ringing in my ears.

I get up with the help of Lacy and Mom. It feels a bit funny to walk again. I don't remember details—I just remember the pain as I got beat. I don't know where the first hit was, or if there was more than one. My mind is fuzzy like an out-of-focus photo. The only thing that's clear, other than the pain, is that Lacy is crying silently, just like my body is doing. Mom helps me back into the bed. I lie down: eyes closed shut, ears ringing loud, and

21

heart beating louder.

"So what are you going to do?" Lacy says through a combination of stifled sobs and sniffs.

Mom's got that tone in her voice like Minister Gibson gets sometimes: old-school hellfire and brimstone. "First step would be for your mama to go up to that police department and file charges or a lawsuit. Whichever one I see fit." I wince. The world seems loud, and I just want quiet.

"I don't think that's a good idea," I whisper. "I don't want this to hover over me."

"What? This already is! Look where you're lying!" Lacy shouts. I motion for her to keep her voice down. "If you don't do something, I will!" she threatens.

"Look. Anger got me here. I don't want that to hold power over my life," I say softly.

I hear the door open and slam; it must be Lex leaving. He wouldn't care about obeying hospital quiet rules. I open my eyes. Mom avoids looking at me; instead, she plays with her wedding ring. She suggests I pray for guidance. It's her answer to everything.

"I think it's best that Bear makes her own decisions. It's up to her what she chooses to do. I'll support her and so will you," Dad states.

"Robert, I can't believe you are letting them get away with this!" Mom argues.

"I hate this too, Tonya, but what do you want me to do? Bomb the police department?! I still have to be alive to walk my baby down the aisle!" Dad pauses and then takes a softer tone. "At this point, it's let go and let God." That's one of his favorite expressions. Neither Mom or Lacy say anything. The room is silent except for the beeping machines taunting me: *do something, do something, do something.*

"Robert, let's talk outside," Mom says, which means they don't want me to see them fight. Once the door closes, it's back to the beeping. I feel Lacy's hands: one of them touches my cheek, the other is holding my left hand. When I squeeze back, tears spill out from both of us. Me, cause I'm in pain, and her, I guess, because she couldn't protect me. Like the coiled snake that's tattooed on my chest, Lacy's ready to strike against any enemy.

ALEJANDRO

"We never got the paperwork, Alejandro,"
says Mrs. Olsen, a Southeast High School
counselor. I sit across from her in her office, at
a desk older than both of us combined.

"They said—" I begin.

But she's not listening. "Even so, I doubt
those credits would transfer."

"They said they would." I hate asking
for help.

She peeks at the computer on her desk, the

phone in her hand. "I'm sorry."

"But I have to go back to school, my caseworker said."

Mrs. Olsen sighs like somebody standing in the cold waiting for a late bus. "I believe your court order would say you have to go to *a* school, not *this* school. With your past, I—"

"Look, I'm done with all that."

Another sigh, this one deeper, like she forgot how to breathe. "Maybe it would be best if you looked at other options like a GED." She won't make eye contact, which is fine with me. I don't need to look at another overdressed, overweight, middle-aged white woman who has no patience with the likes of me.

"I don't want a GED!"

She frowns; it suits her. "If you expect to go to college, then—"

"I want to go into the Marines, like my brother. You need a real diploma, not a GED."

She starts typing on her computer like she doesn't believe me. Or maybe she's just bored.

"Perhaps summer school at one of the district's alternative schools."

I crack the knuckles of my left hand against my head, right by the scar. "Too many bad influences at those schools. I want back in here, to be with Eduardo and the rest my friends and—"

"Alejandro, we need students at Southeast interested in succeeding, not socializing."

"That's me."

She's still typing. Her phone buzzes. And, of course, she sighs.

She picks up the phone. "I need to take this." She starts talking into the phone about lunch plans, so I get up before I go off on her and follow my own plans: *Don't engage, walk away.*

It's the middle of third period, so the halls are kind of empty. Part of me just wants to walk into a classroom, like Mrs. Thomas's English class where we read cool books, or Mr. Perez's science class where he actually taught you how to solve problems, not just memorize a bunch of junk.

I wait around until the bell rings to start lunch, then beeline to my buddy Eduardo's

locker. I hope nobody from my past sees me—
Olishia or 26ers—but I make safe passage.
When Eduardo shows up, I reach out to hug
him and notice his arm in a sling. His right
arm, his throwing arm.

"What happened?" I ask. He doesn't
answer but gives me a look that says it's not
baseball related. He's the varsity catcher, but
at home, mostly what he catches are his Dad's
punches and kicks. I point at the arm. "Look
like we're in the same place. Lost our old
teams, got to find some new ones."

"You get your old schedule back or what?"
he asks, and I tell him, and it's like it used to
be between us. Even though Eduardo wears
a catcher's mitt rather than a 26er tat, we're
closer with more history than I was with any of
those guys. Even when I turned to the streets,
he never turned his back on me or let me
down. We talk until the bell rings.

"I better go," I say. "I don't want you to get
in trouble. Or me."

He nods. "Trouble finds you. But guess
what? You're not the only one." The joy in

27

his voice gets pulled like a plug. He takes out his phone, clicks and clicks. "I wanna show you this."

The video's jumpy, like whoever shot it had a shaking hand. The audio's not much better, but I recognize the voices shouting orders at this young black girl. I can't see her face. Seconds later, I hear the billy club connect, most likely to that girl's skull. I know it's the same cops that got me five days in the hospital and six months in Woodland. The girl hits the ground with a thud, although I can barely hear it over the other girls' yelling.

"What do you think?" Eduardo asks.

I take the phone from his hand, silently memorizing the name LovelyLacyLOL, the person who posted the clip.

"Alejandro?" Eduardo asks.

"I think I have to meet her."

CHRISSIE

"I got you something," Mom says. She hands
me a small package on her way to the kitchen.
I rip open the back like I used to do with
presents on Christmas morning.

It's the new *Call of Duty* Xbox game. I hope
it can relax me, distract me from the pain, but
mostly clear out the memory that serves more
as a never-ending nightmare.

"Thanks, Mom! I've been waiting to
get this!" It's been out for some time; Mom

must've bought it last week after I showed her my report card, mostly A's and a few B's.

"Did you hear from your teachers?" Mom shouts from the kitchen over sounds of her making dinner. My nose perks up, waiting for the smell.

"Yeah. Mrs. Lautner called and said she hoped I'd get better. Mr. Turner said he'd give me an excused pass on our calculus test." I state robotically. School just doesn't seem important now. Nor do those "get well" flowers and cards overfilling the table from every fool boy at Northwest thinking cheap red roses and Dollar Tree sympathy is gonna win me over. I didn't want anything to do with those boys when I was healthy, even less so while I'm healing.

"That's good, sweetheart." She reappears with a bag. "Listen, I found a cute hat at Burlington for you to wear tomorrow when you go back to school! People won't even notice that scar!" Mom says with a smile, like some hat is gonna make a difference.

I touch the bandage on my forehead.

"I'm fixing your favorite cornbread and

stir-fry too—" She's still talking on her way back to the kitchen as I tear the plastic off the game. The sound reminds me of when they pulled the tape off my wrist after the IV. Is everything now going to remind me of the hospital, of my injuries? I turn on the TV, put the game in the Xbox and sit down in the living room, but can't make myself play. I stare at the blank screen acting like a mirror. I don't like what I see in the TV, on or off.

When Mom doesn't hear the game start, she asks, "Chrissie, what's wrong?" She stands at the edge of the kitchen. "Sweetheart?"

I point at the blank black screen. "I can't turn on the TV anymore without someone talking about police brutality or seeing a million videos on YouTube about how the police are the new gang of America!" I pull out my cell phone and flash it at her. I got Lacy to take down the video she put up, the one Robin took, but not before it blew up among my friends. Lacy named me, but the video's so bad, especially once they hit me, you couldn't see the cops' faces clearly.

My cell has been blowing up nonstop with messages from cousins, plus hundreds more people I don't know, leaving their opinion about the situation. Memes, Instagram reactions, Tweets. I feel like a celebrity for all of the wrong reasons. It seems like there's a hundred friend requests from each site and even more direct messages saying how sorry they are for me. How I should pray to God. Links to law documents on my civil rights. Thinking about it overwhelms me; I am not Sojourner Truth or Mary McLeod Bethune or Betty Shabazz. I am Chrissie C. Ross. Normally, I want to be a leader, but not like this. A week ago I was a happy person; now, I'm a hashtag.

Mom doesn't say anything, so I get up, walk over to her and start scrolling. Even as I do, my phone buzzes. Incoming call. Lex. I ignore it.

"I just want to be a regular senior." I say, pouting like I'm seven, not seventeen.

"You should pray," is her answer. She returns to cooking; I stew in my own juices.

I go back to the couch and plop down carefully. I creep up the volume as loud I can stand it and enjoy killing the bad guys in uniforms on *Call of Duty: Advanced Warfare.* I disappear into a game of fiction based on fact. Before I know it, I don't even bother with the nonstop buzzing from my cell phone. My phone notifications blend in with the hail of bullets.

7

"It's gone," Eduardo tells me in between dual-player Xbox action. He's struggling with his busted wing. "The video."

"Why? It was just up yesterday. You save it?" I ask. He shakes his head no.

"You remember the girl's name who posted it?" I nod, not sure how that is going to help. He pulls out his phone. I tell him the name and he looks for other videos she posted.

There are silly videos as well as serious ones

from debate team and clips of Northwest girls' softball. Eduardo clicks to the Northwest web page and looks under athletics, then under girls' softball, and sure enough, there's the girl from the video in the middle row. Lacy Benson. Just as quick, Eduardo finds her on Facebook, but everything's locked down. "Now what?" I ask.

"Who you know at Northwest?" he asks. I start to answer, but stop. "What's wrong?"

I fumble with the controller, killing time, avoiding the obvious. "Only guys I know from Northwest are people I met locked down at Woodland and JDC. Or 26ers. So that's a bad idea."

"Maybe we could go up into the neighborhood and ask—"

I try not to laugh at innocent Eduardo.

"There was one guy I knew in JDC who sucked at basketball worse than me." I don't relish the memory of my feeble attempts to bring my lame game against some icy playground players. "He said he wrestled. I think his name was Curtis something. All mouth, no muscle."

"Got 'em," my fast-fingered friend says with a smile. "Check him out." We look over his Facebook page and not only is it him, but that girl Lacy is in a few of the photos.

Eduardo hands me his phone. "You wanna log on and message him?"

"I deleted my page," I confess. I've told him some of the stuff that Big C and Lorenzo said and did, so he doesn't need to ask why. A bunch of wannabes up to destroy me. I shut everything down and now I'm a digital ghost.

Eduardo's half listening as he's scrolling the guy's page. "This Curtis guy's an idiot. He put his phone number in a post and doesn't have his settings to block it." He shows me the post. I grab a marker off the table and write the digits on my left arm. "You think he'll help?" Eduardo asks.

I pick up the Xbox controller to get my blood racing. "Curtis was in for hitting his mom, but he spent nights crying in his cell. I told him I'd watch out for him. He owes me. Hit 'em up."

***

"Why are you calling me?" Lacy asks when she finally returns my seventh message a little before midnight. Ricardo's not happy to hear the phone ringing this late, but it's not like I have anything else to do, unlike him and Mom who work in the morning. Olsen still won't let me into Southeast, so I'll probably do summer school someplace else. "How'd you get my number?"

I don't snitch on Curtis. "Did you post that vid of the girl hit by the cops?" is all I say.

"How's that your business?" Lacy asks.

"How's the girl? Is she a friend of yours?" I match her query for query. We go back and forth for a while, getting nothing but frustrated with each other. But she doesn't hang up, which gives me hope. "She okay? That looks like a nasty hit she took."

"You tell me why you want to know and maybe I'll tell you something," she says. The snap in her voice has vanished into the night turning into morning. "Don't lie to me."

I sit on the floor in the kitchen, the only

place with a phone with a new number that Mom got to stop Big C's calls. We go back and forth, like Eduardo and me playing catch in the backyard.

"I want to talk to her." All the pressure goes on the word "want."

"She just wants it to go away. I think she's wrong, but—"

"She is wrong. You're right, Lacy." I say firmly, like I just threw a high hard one. "It won't go away if you don't do something, 'cause those two cops will do it again. Trust me."

"I don't know you. Why should I trust you?"

I touch the scar on my head. " 'Cause they did the same thing to me in Powderhorn Park."

She makes a sound like a tire going flat, then says, "Serious?"

"An old white cop with a big scar, and an Asian guy, maybe Hmong, younger, right?"

She doesn't say a word, and I've got her.

"The white cop used the club, right?" More silence. "Lacy, is that what happened to your friend?" I ask. "They hassled her and rather than taking it, she talked back, and it ended with her in a hospital."

More silence, like she's needing all of her energy to think about what to do or say.

"Except for me, they called it resisting arrest, and added on other charges, so after I got out of the hospital, I got placed in Woodland Hills. I'm home and that life's all behind me, except—"

And I let the last word of the sentence hang like bait. She bites. "Except?"

"Except I want to make sure those guys don't get away again." I say each word with clear conviction, just like they taught us in group. "I think you feel the same way."

She says nothing, which says everything.

"Let me talk to your friend. If I had a chance to—"

"She's not gonna listen to somebody she don't even know if she won't listen to—"

"I don't need to say a word," I say hard, fast. "I'm gonna show her the scar on my head."

"That sounds creepy coming from a stranger."

I laugh. "You're right. But I'm practically family now, right? Your friend's blood relative."

"How's that?" she asks.

"We got our skulls crushed by the same cops. Same blood running from our heads."

8

CHRISSIE

"How was the first day of softball practice?"
I ask Lacy. Lacy is team captain, like I was
in basketball. I'm enjoying my senior spring
being sports-free for once. She walks with a bat
strapped on her back and a glove with the ball
inside. She looks like a softball soldier.

"Good. I came out swinging. Sunflower
seeds?" she asks, offering me the bag, which I
turn down. We start to walk, passing different
colors of houses, both well-kept and not. But

most houses we pass on the way home are decent, with kids playing and laughing in the yards.

"My head still is sore." I tell Lacy before she asks.

Today is the last day on my medicine. The doctor said he'll prescribe another refill if the pain comes back. The bright sunlight makes me feel alive and well, but two blocks of silence with Lacy darkens my mood.

"What's wrong?" Lacy finally asks.

"I'm still upset with you. Why did you post Robin's video?" I ask.

We stop and look at each other. Except for the ball and glove, Lacy is my mirror. Light brown eyes with long black hair that curls in the rain. We're two-toned, dark chocolate and peanut butter complexions. She wears her practice uniform; I've got on a short, strapless purple dress. To outsiders, we look different; to us, we're one and the same.

"We all thought that it would be best to share it with the world. To make sure the cops couldn't erase it, because once it's on the

Internet it's out there, permanently. Plus we were beyond the point of being mad about it; we wanted to do something about it, Chrissie, since you—"

"I'm sorry I asked."

"Go ahead and ask! The more questions you ask the more it prepares me for that court room when I get older."

Courts. Law. Police. I want them all to melt away. "Listen Lacy, case closed."

She shakes her head, one hundred percent annoyed. "You thought any more about talking to that guy? Alejandro?" A smirk takes over her face as she smacks the ball into the glove.

"No," I hate lying to my cousin. Ever since she told me about that guy contacting her, it is all I've thought about, which is odd. Since things ended badly with my ex, Reese, I don't obsess over guys. All that desire wasted on guys who aren't loyal. "I don't see what good it will do."

"Well, he wants to meet you. He sounds okay, a little intense, but he gets it."

"Gets it?"

"What you've been through." Lacy points at my head. Mom's purple wool cap covers the scar. "How much longer you gonna cover that thing up? How much longer you going to do nothing? That's not the Chrissie I know and admire. You're a leader. You need to act like one."

"Maybe."

"Who knows, he might just turn out to be cute," Lacy says. "Or better yet, sexy." The way she says the word "sexy" cracks me up, which makes her laugh. She laughs so hard that the ball tumbles. I pick up the ball when it falls on the grass finally free of snow. I hold the ball in my hands fingering the stitches on it, like the ones I got in my head and Alejandro has in his.

We get close to home, which means coming up at the intersection where the police beat me. Lacy gets deathly quiet. The space between us feels heavy and dense.

"Chrissie." Her voice is stern and low. "Me, Robin, and Angela have been so worried about you. You've been distant and different. We can't imagine what you're going through, but remember, you have God and people that care for you."

"God doesn't care." I point at the pavement and slam the ball hard into Lacy's glove. "Why give God credit when he wasn't here."

"You're breathing. Those cops didn't kill you. That speaks volumes. And you need to—"

"Why is everyone telling me what I should do? I know you mean well. But I suggest everyone get beat by the cops and then come back to me with a step-by-step plan for revenge."

"I'm convinced that the law is still just, and we can right this." Lacy says.

"The law did this to me, Lacy. Really . . . how just is it all?" My question falls on particles in the air. Lacy closes the glove around the ball, gripping it tight, keeping it safe. She always likes to try and keep things safe. Is Alejandro that type as well?

ALEJANDRO

"What are you doing up at this hour?" Ricardo asks. I glance at my watch. 5:30 a.m. I pause the Xbox and wait for an answer to arrive from the barrel of my video gun. Nothing.

Not-dad repeats the question.

"Don't know," I answer because, in truth, the reasons I would answer he wouldn't understand. Maybe once, years ago, he obsessed over Mom like I'm obsessing over talking to this girl Chrissie. But I'm guessing

he never had nightmares—well, flashbacks—
of getting beat up, and knowing, dreading,
fearing, somehow oddly wishing the chance
would come again. *This time*, I tell myself, *I'll
fight back. This time*, I shout inside, *I will be
a man.*

"Get to bed, Alex!" Ricardo pulls the
headphone from my ears. He's wearing a
T-shirt too small for his belly; sweatpants too
big for his short legs. He looks like a clown.

And so I let him have it. "Just leave me
alone. I'm busy!"

"Doing what? Playing a game? When I was
your age—" and now it's Ricardo's story time,
telling me about his hard life, like somehow
I've had it easy.

"Fine. I'll go to be bed."

He slaps me hard, but not too hard on the
back of the head. "Alejandro, you made some
mistakes in the past, but that doesn't mean . . ."
and now he sounds like my probation officer
rather than my pretend father. Whatever a
father is supposed to sound like, I don't really
know. The COs at JDC and then later at

Woodland Hills, they all had this tone of "I care about you," but I never believed them. Those were paycheck-based emotions.

"Are you listening to me?" Ricardo asks. I nod yes, an obvious lie.

"Yes, sir." I snap and salute.

"Smart mouth."

"Sorry, that was rude," I whisper.

"Why don't you try getting a job?"

"How I'm supposed do that without a phone?"

He scratches his head, dandruff falls like snow. "I'll leave some money. Get one of those prepaid things so I don't need to worry about it. Don't make it my problem."

For a second I'm not sure what to do with his genuine offer. "Thanks, Ricardo."

He nods, yawns again, and heads off to the kitchen for coffee. I kept my word, shut down the game, and lay in bed. I do nothing other than stare at the ceiling, memorize each inch of it like I did at Woodland. But unlike there, I got something good to think about here: Chrissie.

***

"You Alejandro?" It's a girl's voice, calling just after school would get out. She doesn't sound scared like I am.

"Yeah, is this Chrissie?"

There's a pause like she doesn't want to admit to it. "Yeah. Lacy said I should call you."

"Thanks."

"I didn't want to, but Lacy's my cousin and best friend, so . . ."

Her voice is tiny; she doesn't sound tough like I imagined. "You can't let friends down."

"She tell you what I wanted to talk with you about?" I ask.

"Yeah."

"Can I see you?"

"No," she says quick as a bullet. "How do I know you're not a psycho?"

I laugh, but not like a psycho, and for some reason that makes her laugh. "I like your laugh," I say.

"Thanks."

"After it happened to me, I didn't think I'd ever laugh again. I mean it's not just the pain, but the whole thing just felt like something so wrong in the world, that things would never be—"

"Right again."

"But you get that, don't you, Chrissie." I like the sound of her name.

"Yeah."

"You say 'Yeah' a lot."

"Yeah." Another laugh from me, and that loosens one from her.

And in less than a minute, I feel like I've known this girl my whole life, like a Mr. Perez chem experiment where two elements are joined. Boom! Instant compound! My heart's racing like I'm being chased, but for once in my life, I'm running toward something instead of away.

"So send me a picture so I know what you look like," she requests. "I don't like talking to people if I don't know what they look like."

All I can think is how I'll disappoint her. "I can't." I tell her about not having a phone except the house one. "But I'm going to get a phone today. Soon as I get it, I'll do that. You gonna send me one too?"

"Maybe."

"I like when you said 'Yeah' better."

She's still laughing as she hangs up on me.

***

"Alejandro, bed!" Ricardo says pounding on the door at the stroke of midnight.

"Just a second, Chrissie," I whisper into my new phone. "Ok, Ricardo."

"And stop playing that game all the time!" I've been behind my door since rushing through dinner like my dog Luchador used to with his food, but my hands have been on the phone, not the joy stick.

"Who was that?" she asks. So I tell her about Ricardo, Mil, everything. I tell her, because she asks questions instead of what Olishia did, always talking about herself or telling me what to do or think. We talk about school, family, and *Call of Duty*. We talk about everything but the thing that connects us.

"You gonna send me that photo?" she asks.

I crawl off the bed and huddle in the corner far away from the door, take the photo and send it to her. It's like most any other photos, except I make sure the hair's out of the way so she can see the scar. "Not much to like, right?" I say. She's silent, but answers with a photo of herself. She's striking beyond words. Everything big and beautiful.

"You're fine," I mumble. "Sorry, talking with girls isn't my best thing." She laughs. We keep on as the minutes on my cell click down, stars come out, and my heart aches in a way I never felt before. Has fate played the ultimate trick letting the worst day of my life lead to the best?

10

CHRISSIE

The food on my plate makes me hungrier than
I thought I was. Mashed sour-cream-and-onion
potatoes, asparagus marinated in wine vinegar,
the salad I made with tomatoes and sunflower
seeds, and Mom's specialties: chicken wings
dipped in BBQ sauce and homemade egg rolls.
I feel like I haven't eaten this good in ages, but
as I'm about to begin, Mom motions for my
hand. I grasp hers and Dad's, and we bow our
heads. I play and pray along.

After the prayer, I put a large forkful of the lettuce and bright red tomato in my mouth, and it crunches slowly. The tomato meat rips, and juice explodes in my mouth. My cheek throbs a little. I've just broken my egg roll in half when the doorbell rings.

"I'll get it," Mom says. Dad stops eating; I don't.

"What's up, uncle Ro! It smells good in here," my cousin Lex says way too loud, which is how he always talks. "Hey Auntie Tonya, let me slide in for a minute. I know you have enough." Lex marches inside like he owns this house, as if it was one of the corners he runs for BGD.

"Boy, where are your manners?" Dad says. "We are having a family meal."

Lex stops and throws a hand over his heart, looking injured. "Wow! That hurt. Am I not family? Last time I checked, you married into this family. I share the same blood as Auntie over there." Lex points at Mom, but his penetrating brown eyes fix on my face. The swelling's down, but I take Tylenol as a supplement to meds my doc prescribed.

Though sometimes it feels the pain won't ever stop, like Alejandro said.

"Watch your tone, Lex." Mom says in a motherly order.

"Ya'll know I don't mean disrespect. This is the first time I got the chance to see my young relative since she got out of the hospital." Lex says. He is only three years older than me and Lacy, but he's always acted older than his years. The streets age a person fast. With BGD tats on both arms and one across his neck, Lex looks and lives hard.

He sits down right next to me and starts talking, mainly talking trash about the police, all the while staring me down and helping himself to food that no one offered him.

Mom tries to derail him but doesn't get far. "Lex, we were—"

"Come on, Auntie. I apologize for storming in, but I took the first chance I got." As I listen to his deep raspy voice, I bite into the chicken and his glare is locked on me every time his neck isn't craned low over his plate. The doorbell rings again.

"Who is that, now?" Dad sighs so loud, marching to the door. Lex chuckles and then when Dad opens the door, a female voice booms into our house.

"Lex! You said two minutes. If you were going to chat up a storm, you should have told me! You act like you don't have the sense I raised you with." It's Auntie Dana and behind her is Lacy. Dad invites them in. "Help yourself" must have been written on our front door.

"We can't always show up when we feel like it, Mama," Lacy says. "I told you."

I laugh at the scene playing in front of me: Lacy being all law; Lex being all disorder.

"Child, mind grown folks business. That's my blood sitting in that chair. I can come and go as I please, right Tonya?" Dana says.

"That's right." Mom raises her glass of sweet tea and drinks from it.

"I told you to get money so we could go out to eat." Lacy sounds like she's embarrassed.

"Oh, they'll be alright," Dana says. "We all need to catch up anyway. Fix your mama and yourself a plate. Lex! Get your wannabe muscle-bound butt up and sit on the other side. I have to check on my beautiful niece." Dana gives me a hug and kiss on the cheek.

"Ouch!" I cry. Lex laughs.

"Oh, I'm sorry." Dana sits down in Lex's spot and Lex is across from me eating like he hasn't ate in five days. Dad returns to the table and pulls up a chair for Lacy. Lacy sits and fills a plate for her mom, and one for herself. No doorbell rings.

"How is school, Chrissie?" my auntie asks.

"I can tolerate it now that I've been back for a couple of days. I got an extension on all of my assignments, so I should still graduate on the honor roll this June."

"I love hearing that, honey. 'Me and Lacy, conquering the world!' That's what ya'll used to say when you were little. Do you remember that?" Auntie asks me, grinning from ear to ear.

"Yeah, I remember," I say. Lacy gazes at me with this look that I haven't seen in a long time. Like what I said sparked something in her. She doesn't smile, but it's all in her eyes.

"So you gonna start by taking down the Minneapolis Police?" my auntie asks, no trace of a smile left.

"I'm with you!" Lex says then fills his plate with seconds or maybe thirds.

"Lacy ran home screaming and crying, then Robin showed me that clip! Whoa, I was hot and heated. I had to pray to find my core of peace." Auntie says.

"Me, too." Mom's got nothing but anger and cold in her voice. Dad just continues to eat and doesn't say anything. My scars have become taboo in this house.

"I can't wait to sit in that courtroom and watch you testify," Auntie says. I'm in the middle of drinking cold water when her statement catches me, and I start coughing.

"Mama!" Lacy shouts. The table goes silent except for the sound of Lex chewing, until Lacy lets out a sigh and says, "I told you, Chrissie doesn't want to take this to court."

My auntie turns her head to look at me. "Now, you can't be serious. You got to speak about your story. Baby, you can't run." The fact that no investigators ever found me to get my side of the story told me everything I needed to know: there was no story, just grainy video from a phone on the ground.

"I'm not running! People get beat up every day by the police. Why am I any different? It's just going to be another case anyway." I repeat more or less what I've been saying since I woke up in that hospital, but my voice waivers. Alejandro wants to show me where it happened to him. I'm not sure why, but unlike how I've felt about any other boy ever, I want to see what he has to offer.

Lex pounds his fists on the table. "Doing nothing sends a message that it's alright. We don't let this slide!" He tips over his chair and then storms out the front door, just like he stormed in a few minutes ago, leaving a path of damage. It fits: Lex is a human hurricane.

"Chrissie, listen to me—" Auntie begins.

"That's enough, Dana," Dad intervenes.

"Chrissie, you go tell Lex to get back in here and apologize," Mom instructs me.

I look over at Lacy, hoping she'll take on this task, but she turns away. I know she agrees with Lex that I should do something. It's probably the only thing they agree on anymore.

I leave the table and head toward the front door. Lex's foot is tapping on the sidewalk fast and loud like a woodpecker working a tree. "Lex, I just want to live my life, which means letting this go. That's how I can beat this."

He shows his face and blows out a smoke ring. "Lacy probably hasn't told you this, and don't mention it to her. She cried for two days after she left the hospital with y'all. Since then, she's been reading law books. But I'd rather get my information the way the streets provide it. Then it's authentic."

I think about the hard lessons that Alejandro said he learned on the streets. "But, Lex."

"Point is, Lacy hasn't slept. When she does sleep, it's only for an hour." He shook his head and met my eyes again. "Stop being selfish. This doesn't just affect you—it affects the people who love you. If you haven't noticed already, in this country people are starting to understand a portion of what it's like to be black. I'm tired of seeing cops act like a fake military with no one fighting back!"

His brown eyes look cold, but I know he's burning hot as the blackie he's smoking. "I'll do anything to send a message that they aren't going to just rough you up and get away with it. And I'll have my girlfriends with me." He mentions his girlfriends sometimes when he talks about street business.

His girlfriends are his Berettas.

11

ALEJANDRO

"This is where it happened," I tell Chrissie.
We're at Powderhorn Park, where the
basketball courts are crowded and rowdy.
Yet the second Chrissie got off the number-
five bus, no other sight or sound mattered.
She's more beautiful in person, which seems
scientifically impossible.

"Do you really want to talk about it?"
Chrissie asks. Her voice is poetry in motion.

I nod, strong and determined. "In group, at

Woodland, they told us the only way to work through anything was to talk, 'cept when I talked about it there, nobody got it."

"That's why I didn't want to talk about it or want Lacy to post that video," Chrissie says. "I just want it to go away."

"It won't," I counter. "And that's the worst part, 'cause it's like they still got control over my life."

When she moves her arm, I try to see if she's got a tat. She's free at least on the little bit of skin she's showing. She's got to know about me. "Like my old gang."

She's quiet, which makes the noise around us seem louder somehow. "Old, like no more?" she confirms.

I nod, but I don't say anything. According to me I'm out, but according to Big Caesar and Lorenzo, I'm still in. Which I don't get since they jump in new people all the time. All it takes is finding the right person at the wrong time in their life, and next thing you know, the 26ers are your new best friends.

"Alejandro." She waves her left hand in

front of my face. She's got her nails painted with sparkly stuff, with the same kind of sparkle around her eyes.

"Sorry, I get lost in my thought some times."

"Me too."

We keep walking and talking about nothing much, but it seems like every minute, one of us says "me too." When we get closer to the field house, she's doing most of the talking.

"Here." I stop her, point toward the field house. "Back there."

I start walking, but she's not coming with me. "You still don't trust me, do you?"

She stands still, arms crossed.

I turn and walk back toward her. "Chrissie, I never want to cause another person in this world any pain. I mean, except—"

"Except."

"Except the two cops that beat me."

I wait for her to say "me too," but she doesn't this time; she doesn't say anything.

I reach out my left hand. "Trust me, please." She hesitates; I move closer. "Trust me."

Our fingers touch but don't interlock. "Here's what happened."

I tell how we were getting high after a day of making money for those above us. About the cops coming up on us, about Big Caesar and Lorenzo acting all tough, talking back. About the cops telling us to turn around and me snapping, tired of people—Big C, Olishia, teachers, cops, Ricardo, everybody—telling me what to do. I tell her about the orders from the cops, but mostly that black club they used. Big C and Lorenzo pushing me while they took off like it was my duty to take their beating.

"Last thing I remember is seeing the club come toward my head while my friends deserted me. Or, people I thought were friends. After that, it's all blackness until waking up in the hospital and seeing my mom crying."

I'm not crying, but close. I'm about to say something, but then she wraps her fingers around mine. "So, believe me when I say you can trust me," I whisper. "Can I trust you?"

She stays quiet, but when she nods and kisses me, it's all the answer I need.

12

A first kiss turns into a second and then into
too many to count.

There are too many similarities between
us. His eyes show a pain that he can't speak,
and I know all too well. That's why when
my hand pulls him close and our lips meet,
the concepts of space and time become
nonexistent. My mind won't shut down, caught
up in confusion and passion.

I snap out of it, feeling almost light-headed

from all the blood racing through my veins.

"I have to go." I step back. "I'm sorry," I say as I start to walk away from him.

"Chrissie, wait." He touches my arm softly. His voice and his light brown eyes are hard to resist. It takes all of me to stay put.

"Why are you—" he starts.

I cut him off. "We can't do this," a whisper of fear and doubt from deep within speaks for me. "I don't lose myself in boys like so many girls. I did once, never again—"

"Why can't we?" he asks as he holds my hand tighter. "Is this because I'm Latino? Is it about my past?"

"No, it's just that—" I cut off. I don't know what to say. Is it because he was in jail or in a gang? Or am I afraid of the dark path that desire can take a person down? I don't know.

"I'd better go." I start to walk off again.

"Chrissie, wait." He stops me with his words, and I turn to face him. Is it weird that I don't really hear or see anything else but him? I take off my hat, and he inhales.

He gently kisses the scar of my forehead.

"I feel like I know you. Please just trust me, please." Alejandro is so sexy when he is serious. His eyes lock me in again.

"A kiss seals the deal." I say. We smile and share another kiss, perhaps our most important. We walk hand-in-hand away from the scene of the crime committed by the police.

"Can I ask one more thing?" I whisper. Hands and lives entwined.

He nods.

"What part of *Advanced Warfare* are you on?"

He laughs at my question and we're both smiling as we walk and talk about *Call of Duty*.

ALEJANDRO

"It was nice to meet you," Chrissie tells Mom and Ricardo as I walk her out the door.

"You don't need to lie to my folks," I whisper, and she laughs. Ricardo actually let me borrow the car to pick her up and take her home, though I'm not sure it makes up for what they did during dinner. They grilled Chrissie more than Mom did the skirt steak we ate.

Chrissie takes my hand. "I've been through worse interrogations."

"Me too," I point to my scar. "'Cept I don't remember most of it." I walk over, open up the car door for Chrissie, like Ricardo used to do for Mom.

As soon as Chrissie sits, I kiss her. I should've waited until I was sitting too since I feel my heart racing and knees buckling.

"Alex, come here!" Ricardo shouts from the front door. Knowing he's watching, I hold the kiss. I could tell from the get-go, he didn't like Chrissie. Mom not so much either. They already say I spend too much with her, but they don't know that only forever would be enough.

I break the kiss. "Be right back."

I stomp inside the house. "What?"

"This is a bad idea, Alex, very bad." Mom's arms are crossed. Ricardo stands behind her.

"You just met her!" I shout.

"So did you," Mom reminds me. "This is too much too soon, you need to focus on—"

"But I love her." These words escape my lips with ease.

Ricardo laughs. "You don't know the meaning of the word, son."

He doesn't know it either, and I hate when he calls me son. "I love Chrissie."

More laughter from Ricardo, and a hard stare in return from me. "You kids use words like *love* and *loyalty* like you know what they mean. If you loved her, Alex, you wouldn't leave her alone in the car. You'd protect her always," Ricardo the Oracle pronounces as law.

"You called me in here," I remind him.

"We know that—" Ricardo starts, and my stare rests on Mom. She turns away, examines the dinner table like Judas at the Last Supper. And Ricardo goes on using that word "we" like they've decided my life for me. He ends by telling me, "You should focus on your responsibility to be a good son and a soldier of Christ, instead of lusting after another ghetto girl you barely know."

"You don't know anything about me, or about her, but especially about us!"

Ricardo sighs like he got punched in the gut; I'll aim lower.

"Ricardo, maybe when you marry my mom

and earn your keep, then you can lecture me about responsibility to our family—"

"Watch your step, son."

"She and I are the same person. We've shared the same experience. It binds us like wire."

Ricardo takes a step toward me, and I clinch my fist. But he doesn't throw a punch or give me the back of his hand, he clutches my right arm over my 26ers tat. "So one day you're loyal to your thug friends, that girl Olishia, and now to the first new girl who bats her big brown eyes at you."

"She's not some girl." I look over to Mom, avoiding Ricardo's dismissive glare.

"Loyalty and honor don't work like that," Ricardo retorts. He huffs and puffs, but he won't blow my house down. "They are not words you say, they are things you do."

"Alejandro," Mom says, "loyalty is love in action."

"And what should I do?" I pull my arm away. Ricardo starts to answer, but I cut him off 'cause I know he's got no answers. "Rejoin the 26ers?"

He shakes his head. Mom looks up, tears in the corner of her eyes.

"But you don't want me to be with Chrissie."

Another head shake from Ricardo.

"Look, I'm trying to be a good kid like Eduardo, but it's hard." What's harder, though I don't say it, is that Eduardo's not returning my calls lately. Last we talked, I'd just told him about meeting Chrissie.

"Try harder," is Ricardo's predictable comeback.

"So what is it, Ricardo? What should I do?"

Our small house echoes with the roar of silence, broken quickly by my racing out the door, back into the car, and then driving with Chrissie into the heart of the dark night. She asks nothing of me, and that is why she can have everything.

14

"What's wrong?" I'm next to him in his stepfather's car, fixed on his worried eyes.

"Nothing." Alejandro turns up the music.

"You ran out of your house," I say, "Slow down and talk to me." But it's just music as he drives toward my house. When we're close, he pulls into an empty lot, one of many. We're surrounded by nothing but each other and a quiet northside night without blaring sirens.

He stares at the floor. "Mom and Ricardo

say . . . we spend . . . too much time together."
For the first time I can remember, he fumbles
with his words. My parents don't feel that way
because they don't even know about him. It has
to be that way. They think I'm out with my
friends when I'm with Alejandro.

"Do you have to stop seeing me? If that's
what you need, OK. But what is this really
about?" I ask. "Do you *want* to stop seeing
me?" I feel everything inside coil and tighten.

"No! You know I love you. But . . ." he
drifts off into nothing. A bus rumbles past.

"You found me from a video!" We're face
to face, and my hands wave in the air. "You tell
me to trust you, and now you don't know what
you want because your family tells you what to
do. Where does your loyalty lie?"

"My family doesn't know what they are
talking about. They think they know, but they
don't." Alejandro turns away and tightens his
grip around the steering wheel, choking it.

"I don't understand. You tell me to trust
you, and now after all we've shared, you say you
don't know. How do you let someone control

you so easily? I really want to know," I ask.

"No one controls me, but me," Alejandro says. I think that's how I used to feel, until those cops beat me down with hate.

"Yeah, right. I get what I want, and I want you. But I guess you don't want me," I say.

"I do. But . . ." he drifts off once more.

"But you need to make up your mind! I have to know if you are in this without a doubt. If you are wasting my time, what's the point?"

He has no response. He tries kissing me, but I'm not having it. I got a hundred guys who wanna kiss me, but that's not what I need. "If you're going to break my heart, Alejandro, you'd better know something."

"Chrissie, I'm just confused. So much so soon. I've never felt this way before."

"I have, sort of," My stomach rumbles at the memory of Reese. "I won't let it happen again." As I say the words, I know it's not only about getting my heart broken. I'm wondering why I don't feel the same about protecting other folks from getting beat by those cops like Alejandro and me were.

15

"Everything's new," Chrissie whispers to me.

We're lying in Powderhorn on our jackets on the first sixty-degree day of spring, which brings the whole city outside. After the hour we spent kissing, I lost track of time. We've spent the rest of the afternoon talking about how, because we share a past, we can build a future together. I told her I didn't care what anybody said, not even my Mom. All I desired in the world was Chrissie.

"It's like anything's possible," I whisper back, then pull her right next to me. Her tank tops are hanging low, and that's when I see it. "You have a tattoo!"

She pulls down her strap enough for me to see the full thing. It sits just above her heart.

"What's the story?"

She hesitates, so I wait.

"So, ever since I was young, I always loved snakes. I'd be fascinated with the patterns of their skin and how they would shed. I think they are beautiful and the way they move so slick; I admire that trait from them."

I look again. "Two snake heads with their scaled bodies," I make out.

She nods. "They're entangled in each other, and made of chain coils."

"Wow."

"I know, it's a lot of symbolism." She takes my hand and traces the tattoo. "I used to always let people tell me what to do. But then I liked the idea that I could, kind of, shed my skin. Be powerful on the inside. So I got this tattoo. Feels like it helps protect me.

"You think I'm crazy now that I told you this," she says, smiling.

"You're not crazy. You're strong. There's a difference."

She squeezes my hand as we lie there, peaceful. We stay that way, just beating heart to heart, letting the sun shine down on us like seeds waiting to grow.

Then suddenly there's no more sun, just a dark shadow. Make it two. Big C and Lorenzo.

"Chrissie, don't move," I whisper, pull her tighter. I wonder if she feels my hands shaking. "A couple of my old crew are here. Let me handle it."

She rolls over, stands up, and readjusts her blue jeans and dual purple tanks which I did a fine job of rearranging. I rise, stand in front of her, and try to relive the part I once played.

"Who is this?" Big C asks. I don't like how he's examining Chrissie with his eyes.

"She's none of your business," I shoot back.

"Speaking of business," Lorenzo says. "When you coming back to work for us?"

"*We* are 'us' now," I say loud and clear. "Not you."

Big C snorts. "You said that about my sis too." Lorenzo slaps his hands together in joy.

"Sister. His sister?" Chrissie sputters and then takes a deep breath.

Big C belly laughs. "A-hole didn't tell you about him and Olishia hooking up."

Before I can say a word, Chrissie turns her back and retreats. Big C howls like this is the funniest thing he's ever seen. "Chrissie, wait up!" I yell as her fast walk turns into a run. As I race after her, the sounds and smells of the park intensify. I'm in the present.

I catch up with her and put my hand on her shoulders. "Chrissie, let me explain." She doesn't turn around. "There was nothing with Olishia, not like with you."

She pulls my hands off her bare shoulders and buries her face in her hands. I get in front of her and apologize for not telling her about Olishia. "I never loved her," I insist.

Chrissie drops her hands and puts them in mine. She squeezes my hands, soft at first and then hard to the point where it hurts. "Was she smarter than me? More beautiful? Did she do things to you that I won't?" I'm surprised Chrissie's brown eyes don't turn green as the jealous monster within her rises to the surface.

"There is no one smarter or sexier or stronger than you," I whisper. "You do something for me that Olishia never could. You give me a reason to wake up every morning."

She releases my hands and puts hers in front of her mouth as she takes deep breathes to calm herself. "So he was just saying that to hurt me?" Chrissie finally makes eye contact with me.

"To hurt us," I remind her. "Like I said, there is no me and you, there is just us."

Her breathing regulates. But the green of envy I sense, as I watch her hands ball into fists, is losing to red rage and her desire to be the white knight in shining armor. And just as quickly as she retreated from the battlefield, she walks back toward where Big C and Lorenzo still stand.

They point at us, hands tilted like they were pointing pistols. They mock fire. Chrissie advances. She stands eye to eye with Big C. I try to get between them, but she pushes past.

Her eyes narrow. Her voice is loud and clear. "These were the two that let you take a beating from those cops, right?" I nod. "Must be stupid and weak."

"Watch your mouth!" Big C yells in her face.

"They ran, so why should we walk away from them?" she shouts over my shoulder.

I'm trying to think of a good reason, but it's hard to think with all the smack Big C and Lorenzo are talking. They drop every b-, c-, and f-bomb in the book. Chrissie doesn't flinch.

"What you gonna do, run away again?" Chrissie yells out.

"What are you gonna do?" Big C says. I try to pull her back, but she's not having it. She doesn't see Big C or Lorenzo, I bet, but those two cops who insulted and then beat her.

Lorenzo starts squawking, but Chrissie talks over him. "You're really going to beat up a female in public with a hundred people with phones to film it so you can get your butts behind bars where you belong? And only one of you cowards will do time. Who's going to snitch first?"

"A-hole, you best tell your woman—" Lorenzo starts.

"His name is Alejandro, and I'm Chrissie." She's got no fear in her voice. "Do you know who I am?" They stand there looking dumb and stunned.

"My cousin Lex runs a BGD crew," she says, which is scary news to me. "You run blocks because they let you. You live because they let you. You touch me or Alejandro, his family or friends, then your mommas are going be going to a funeral. Do you understand me?"

They're silent until Big C whispers to Lorenzo, who tells Chrissie, "I don't believe you."

"Feel free to test my statements. I don't believe a word you say. Who leaves their *'brother'* 26er to take a hit?" Chrissie lies back down on the grass and motions for me to join her. I turn my back on the 26ers and face my one and only, on the ground next to her.

I whisper, "They still there?"

"No, but I am," she whispers to me. And I know nothing else matters.

16

CHRISSIE

As Alejandro drives me home, I can tell something's bothering him again. "What's wrong?" I whisper.

"I should have stood up for you, not the other way around," he mumbles.

"You stepped up before, and what did you get for it?" I look at his scar and then squeeze his arm tight. "It's me and you."

"How'd this happen?" he asks.

"What? Us?" The weight of those

two letters feels heavy yet uplifting at the same time.

We ride in silence until he rests a hand on my leg. "We're here—that's what matters."

I can't hold in what I'm thinking. "I'm scared that what brought us together will tear us apart."

He slows down and eases the car toward the side of the road. "Nothing will tear us apart."

He leans over and kisses me. For a long time, we just hold onto each other like two people tossed overboard from a sinking ship, hanging on for dear life. It feels right.

Everything's perfect until my phone rings. "It's Lacy." I answer it and listen as she talks fast. I can't believe what I'm hearing. When I hang up, I smack the dash of the car so hard the glove box pops open.

"What's wrong?"

I turn to look at him but can only get out one word. "Another."

"Another what?"

"They found him in his house, but Lacy

tells me, his injuries look the same as mine. Up northside, my people, just a few blocks from here."

"You think that—"

"I know it's them, Alejandro. How many broken skulls is it going to take?"

He pulls me closer. "I know you don't like people saying you got to speak up for everyone, like it's your obligation to them. It's not about what you owe them. It's something stronger."

"Justice." We say the word together as he pulls back onto the road.

I read texts that keep pouring in from Lacy as Alejandro drives fast, matching the adrenaline no doubt racing through his veins. What kind of justice will finally right these wrongs? If it's street justice, dues are paid in blood. But is that what I want? More blood?

What I need is help from one of the smartest people I know. I call Lacy back. Alejandro looks my way and stares hard at the road in front of us. He looks like a captain of a warship.

As Lacy gives me the details, I'm gripping the phone so tight I don't know how it's not breaking in half. "Yeah . . . we'll meet you guys where it happened . . . yeah. It was them! Okay, we're on our way."

"What?" Alejandro says after I end the call.

"Curtis Washington from Northwest."

"The guy I knew from JDC, Lacy's friend?"

It's hard to speak with my jaw clenched so tight. "His condition wasn't given out to the press, but I'm sure it's critical." My phone buzzes and the text reads, "Time to do something." It's from Lex. He's right, but not his way. I bury myself in thought until an idea comes to me.

My eyes widen as I look out the windshield. "Alejandro. I have a crazy idea. Will you help me?"

"I'm here. You didn't have to ask."

"We're going to provoke another incident, film it, and then go public."

He studies me for a second. "You sure? Last time with you, you made Lacy take it down," he reminds me.

"I know. That was a mistake," I admit. I thought not having it out there would help put me past it and not have it define me, but I was wrong. Until I know these cops won't crack another skull, then I'll never be over it. "We can't make our past become somebody else's future."

"What about after it's out there for the world to see?" he asks me.

"We go on with our lives while the cops rot in jail. We finish school, and then get jobs and rent an apartment together."

He smiles wide, which fades into a smirk. "You could be onto something."

I can see myself with him for the rest of my life. Something about him calms me—but also inspires me.

I text Lacy, Robin, and Angela to ask for their help. They each say "yes," and all I can think to reply is "I love you."

I put my head with all my racing thoughts on Alejandro's shoulder. The miles tick while my brain moves ten times our speed. We head forward to face our past.

17

"Here," Chrissie says. I slow the car down as we pull over near a vacant lot off Broadway.

It looks like any other vacant lot on the northside or around Powderhorn. Across the street, there's police tape around Curtis's house indicating a crime scene. Except we know the criminals are the police.

"What next?" I ask. That's the problem with following your heart; it leaves only questions, where duty and responsibility give you answers. It's easier to be a soldier or prisoner than a free man making hard choices.

Chrissie picks up her phone and starts looking through her contact list. If she's like me, she's got people she calls when she's in trouble, and she's got people she calls who *are* trouble.

As we drive, I overhear her explaining her plan once more to her friends when my phone rings. Eduardo, finally.

"What's up?" he asks. "Where you at?"

"No place, just driving around."

"Meet me at Chrissie's. Gimme the address, I need to talk to you in person." Eduardo sounds scared. I try to talk more, but he just keeps asking for the address.

I rattle off the address and try to catch up about his life without baseball, but he cuts the call short. We head to Chrissie's place, where I park the car and walk her toward her front door. The lights are off. Eduardo said he'd meet me here, but I don't see him.

The front steps are as far as I get before I hear it. The screech of the brakes.

Then the *bang bang bang* of bullets. The shots miss us and hit her house.

We run behind her house and into the alley. In the distance, I hear a door slam and an engine rev. Through back alleys and vacant lots, Chrissie and I run for our lives.

"This way!" I yell. I circle around in front of her house. "Go inside!" I shout as I race for Ricardo's car.

"I'm coming with you," she replies, and we jump into the car. Seconds later, I hear the roar of a car. Impala. Big C. As I'm escaping, I ask Chrissie to call Ricardo. She hands me the phone, and we talk in Spanish so Chrissie can't understand. I tell him what's happening; he tells me what to do. I'm talking way too fast, like I'm driving, but he's calming me down.

I think about just driving into a police station, but what if those cops are there, or ones like them? Can I ever trust the police again? If not, how can I escape Big C and Lorenzo?

I make the drive from Chrissie's house to mine in record time. We race from the car toward the front door. Somewhere along the way I lost Big C, but they know where I live.

My hands shake as I reach for my keys. I drop the keychain, but Chrissie picks it up, puts it in the lock, and we race inside. Before I can say a word, Ricardo speaks.

"Alex, son, you okay?" Ricardo asks and in four words, four years of his indifference and impatience don't matter anymore. Mom's beside him, crying.

"They're on their way," I manage to say through heavy breathing.

"How many?" Ricardo asks.

"I think just Big Caesar and Lorenzo," I answer.

"Chrissie, Rosalie, you get into the bathroom. Stay safe! Close the door!" Ricardo shouts. Mom starts toward the bathroom, but Chrissie stands still like a statue.

"Alex, you ready to defend what you love?" Ricardo asks.

I stare at Chrissie. "Yes."

Ricardo nods and leaves the room, and so do I. A few seconds later he emerges carrying a hunting rifle. I've got my .45 from the baseball card box. I grasp it like a long-lost relative.

"They got two," Ricardo says. "We got a .22 and a .45."

"And 911," Chrissie says. Mom's behind her, trying to pull her to safety, but she's sticking by me. I clutch the pistol in my right and her hand in my left. Our fingers wrapped like barbwire.

"Call," I say, and Chrissie dials 911 on her cell. Outside we hear a car pull up and a car door open. Mom and Chrissie hit the floor, while Ricardo and I move toward the window. I peek out between the curtains. The Impala. Three, not two, sets of legs get out of the car. Five arms, because one of the people exiting the car has his arm in a sling. Eduardo.

It's like I feel the slicing jab of a knife in my back as I back away from the window and bang my head against the wall, repeating the words, "No, Eddie, no."

My breaking heart beats faster as we all wait to see if the police will come to help rather than hurt. Will they do their duty?

18

"You're sure you still want to do this?"
Alejandro asks me. Police that were more
"civil" came and took Big C and Lorenzo away
before any shots were fired. Good citizens and
good cops don't need bad police officers, and
it's our time to fight back the right way.

"Positive." I pound my hand into my first,
but when we pull up to the spot I feel tranquil.

"Alejandro, if anything happens . . ." then I
lose my words, and we get out of Ricardo's car.

I shut the door and walk. I haven't ever been more in the moment than I am right now.

"What's wrong?" He rubs my arm.

I hesitate. *God gave me a purpose. I got to do something.* My face tightens at the question that follows: *If God exists, why doesn't* He *do something?*

"Chrissie, I said is there something I can do?" Alejandro asks, but I'm tripping.

"Follow through." I say, and we walk up to Lacy. The spot's right between the corner where I got beat and Curtis's house, where those same two cops hurt him. I glance at the bushes directly to my left and then back at Lacy. This neighborhood is their beat, and their beat-down area.

"Lacy. Meet Alejandro," I say. Seeing my favorite people shake hands makes me crack a smile. I wish Robin and Angela were here too, but they're already busy with their roles in this operation.

"So we're all clear," I ask, "Angela already called the police, so they should be on their way, right?"

Lacy nods her head up and down.

"Good. And me and Alejandro will provoke them while you film them from behind those bushes, but Robin will be across the street filming too."

Lacy nods and hides behind the bushes. Alejandro and I hold hands tightly and wait.

It takes less time than I imagined before a squad car pulls up. My heart beats so quickly. They flash their headlights and get out. We're in the spotlight. It's our time.

"Look it. It's that girl," The Hmong cop says to the old white guy.

"We know it was you that beat up Curtis last night," I say. "He's in the ER with a broken skull. Your signature touch." I throw off mom's cap and point to the scar on my head.

"You don't know anything," the white cop says, walking closer. "You think we owe you all something because of your ancestors? That the whole world should give you special treatment and let you keep running our neighborhoods into the ground?"

"Watch your mouth." Alejandro and I say at the same time.

"I don't have to watch anything. I'm an officer of the law. I'm the one wearing a badge. I make the calls." Like a snake, the white cop spits venom when he opens his mouth.

The Hmong cop raises his club toward me. I put my hands up but don't back away.

"Hit her and I swear you won't breathe again!" Alejandro yells while he holds me tight.

I can feel the vibrations of his voice shake on me. I look up at him and something shifts in his eyes. *Alejandro, don't do anything too brash. Please*, I think to myself. *Just do like you told me about getting out of Woodland Hills.* "Stick to the plan." I say to him.

Alejandro starts breathing heavy—too heavy. "You wanna hit someone, hit me."

The cops look at each other, and laugh. "Hey, I remember you. We already did!"

I watch Alejandro's chest, watching to see if he'll make a move. He takes a step toward the Hmong cop who smashes the club against his knee; the white cop kicks me in the stomach.

We're both on the ground, but just for a
second. Alejandro loses it. He dives at the
Hmong cop, tackles him. He gets behind him
and starts choking him. The officer looks like
he's struggling and trying to fight him off. The
white cop calls for backup in his walkie-talkie.
I gather strength and stand up straight.
Everything is sudden and quick but also in
slow motion. The white cop pushes me back
down and pulls Alejandro off his partner, but
the Hmong cop doesn't move. It's a real fight,
not some stunt now, but all I can hope is Lacy
and Robin are filming every second.

"Cancel backup," the white cop says into
the talkie. He reaches into his sock. He pulls
out a small pistol and throws the weapon
at Alejandro. "Deadly force allowed when
an officer feels threatened by a perp with
a weapon."

Alejandro looks at the gun, but I kick it
away. How did our desire for justice cloud
our judgment so badly? Alejandro starts to
go for the gun, and the white cop reaches for
his weapon.

"You should rethink that action!" comes a booming voice from the darkness. Lex. He must have followed Lacy. He holds Berettas in both hands as he stands next to me.

The white cop puts his hands in the air. "I won't need you to beat me over the head before I make my move on ya'll pigs!" Lex shouts.

"Lacy, leave!" I yell to her, "Now!"

"I'm not going anywhere." Lacy says emerging from the bushes. I turn and she runs toward us. I don't want her to get hurt. I want her to save someone's life someday.

"Leave, sis. This is about to get ugly, and if you die I might as well die too," Lex states like a man who could care less about life and death.

"No, Lex, I—" Lacy starts, but Lex motions for her to leave. He's got one eye on his sister, the other on the white cop, when it happens.

"Drop your weapon!" the Hmong cop yells. He's on one knee, pistol in hand.

"Drop yours! You didn't think it would come to this, did you? Trust me, I got fire for you." Lex says. "Go home, Chrissy. I got this."

"No, *we* got this," I whisper, knowing that Robin is still filming. "Leave, Lacy!"

Lex starts singing, "I shot the sheriff, but I did not shoot the deputy!"

"Lex put the guns down, they aren't worth it." I say in a steady tone. Lex's eyes dart back and forth between the officers. Alejandro bends over and picks up the piece the white cop had used as bait and points it right at the guy's scared and scarred face. I swear everything is silent.

I take slow steps and meet eyes with the white cop, whose stare at me is lethal. "What makes you hate me so much?" I ask him.

He answers with racist trash talk, disrespecting me and everyone of my skin, like nothing I've ever done or could ever do matters. That anything I could achieve was garbage. That *I* was garbage, some weak and powerless black girl. He don't have a clue.

I snatch the gun from Alejandro's hand. He and Lex yell, "Chrissie, no!" as I point and fire, but the trigger clicks against an empty chamber. The white cop draws his weapon before I can react.

Bang Bang Bang Bang Bang Bang!

The bullet is hot when it hits me in the chest. The grass feels cool as I fall on my side. My eyes open and close to see the Hmong cop go down, then Lex, and then the white cop. I find the urge to close my eyes growing after the blasts stop.

"Lex!" Lacy shouts, and I see her run to Lex. She's moving fast; he's perfectly still.

Alejandro crawls next to me. "Chrissie." He takes off his shirt and presses it against the snake tattoo on my chest that failed to protect me. Blood spouts up from me, but I sense it running down on me from him as well. "Chrissie, stay with me, we can make it!"

"I'm sorry, Alejandro, I just wanted—" There's no energy in me. I just want to go to sleep now. I don't feel the coldness of the grass anymore. I don't feel pain or anything. Numb.

"Chrissie, hold on." Alejandro's breathing is labored.

"Alejandro . . ." My head holds no weight. I push all the energy toward my tongue. "Yea though I walk through the valley of the shadow

of death I shall fear no evil for You *are* with
me. Your rod and Your staff they comfort
me . . ." I mumble. Before I close my eyes I
see a snake that slithers by, crawling from my
chest. My eyes open to see a blade of grass.
They close. Open. Close. Open.

19

"Chrissie, no!" I shout into her ear, inches from my mouth. A mouth with blood trickling out. I know she can't hear me or see me. Her eyes are open, vacant, unmoving.

"Lex! Lex!" Behind me, I hear Lacy scream. In the distance, I hear sirens coming too late. My insides burn with pain from bullets imbedded too deep in my body.

"It was my job to protect you," I mumble to Chrissie.

"I called 911 again," I hear some girl say, her voice growing louder, closer.

"Lacy, are you all right?" Another girl shouts.

I'm face down, half of me on the ground, the other half draped over Chrissie's prone body. My head rests on her wound. I pretend she's the snake, wrapped around my body, forcing life into me.

"Chrissie, it's Angela and Robin! Chrissie!" They shout and cry, over and over again.

"Alejandro, you're going to make it," Lacy bends down, sobbing, touching my face with one hand. She clutches my hand with the other. I can't squeeze back. I can't tell her I know she's lying to me.

"Did you . . . get . . . the video?" I force the question out to Lacy.

Lacy nods. Between crying gasps, she whispers, "I got it all."

"Robin and me were across the street, with her camera," Angela says, looking furious but wiping an endless stream of tears. "God, Chrissie. We'll get justice."

My mind's cloudy, yet somehow never clearer. Justice is hot and cold. My blood runs hot from my wounds; Chrissie's body starts to cool. I gather my energy and pull myself so we're face to face. Her open eyes stare at me. I close them and kiss them, and I know I'm glad I didn't walk away from her—that I did engage. I didn't follow the plan. I followed my heart. Her heart. Our hearts soon to beat together forever.

ABOUT THE AUTHORS

Patrick Jones is the author of more than twenty novels for teens. He has also written two nonfiction books about combat sports, *The Main Event*, on professional wrestling, and *Ultimate Fighting*, on mixed martial arts. He has spoken to students at more than one hundred alternative schools, including residents of juvenile correctional facilities. Find him on the web at www.connectingya.com and on Twitter: @PatrickJonesYA.

Marshunna Clark is a young African American writer based in the Twin Cities of Minnesota. She wrote her first book in collaboration with a friend at age sixteen to combat the summer "I'm bored" syndrome, and her interest in various storytelling formats led her to pursue a degree in screenwriting at Minneapolis Community and Technical College.